First published in the UK in 2016 by Tiny Owl Publishing Ltd, London

Based on a story in Shahnameh by Ferdowsi
Retold by Ali Seidabadi
Illustrated by Marjan Vafaian
Edited by Nicolette Jones
Translated by Azita Rassi
Graphic designer Elahe Javanmard

ISBN: 978-1-910328-14-9
A CIP catalogue record for this book is available from the British Library.

tiny owl publishing

Bijan & Manije
Ali seidabadi
Marjan Vafaian
Edited by Nicolette Jones

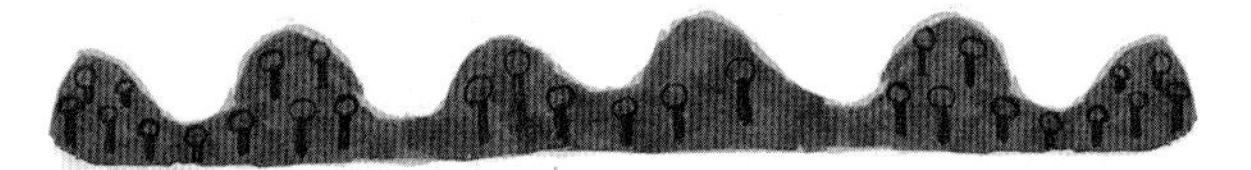

Once upon a time the people of Iran and the people of neighbouring Turan were enemies. Turan was ruled by a tyrant, King Afrasaib, who made his subjects tremble and threatened the country next door. Iran was a land of colour and perfume and beauty, ruled over by good King Khosrow.

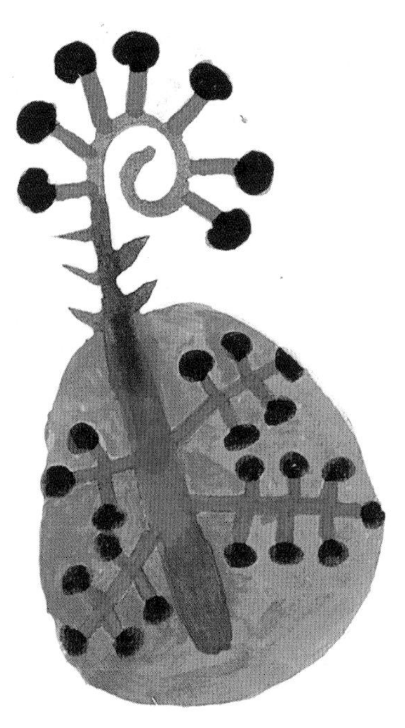

One day at Khosrow's court, a splendid feast was interrupted by a messenger. "I come", he said, "from the Armenians, who live by the border with Turan. The forest there has been overrun by monstrous wild boars, with tusks like granite, trampling our crops and toppling trees. Please help us, good king." Khosrow piled a gold tray with jewels and offered it to the knight who would be brave enough to drive the boars away.

A valiant young man stepped forward. His name was Bijan.

The King, fearing his champion was too young, commanded the head of his army to go with Bijan to keep him safe. But when they reached the forest, General Gorgin took fright. He left the youth to do battle with the boars alone.

Bijan was clever. It was hard to catch boars in a forest, where they could be lost among the trees. So he hid himself within sight of a waterhole, and waited. When the thirsty boars gathered to drink, he rushed upon them with ropes. He pursued them like a lion, and as they scattered, their tusks struck sparks from the rocks. But Bijan was tireless and swift, and soon he had tied them all together.

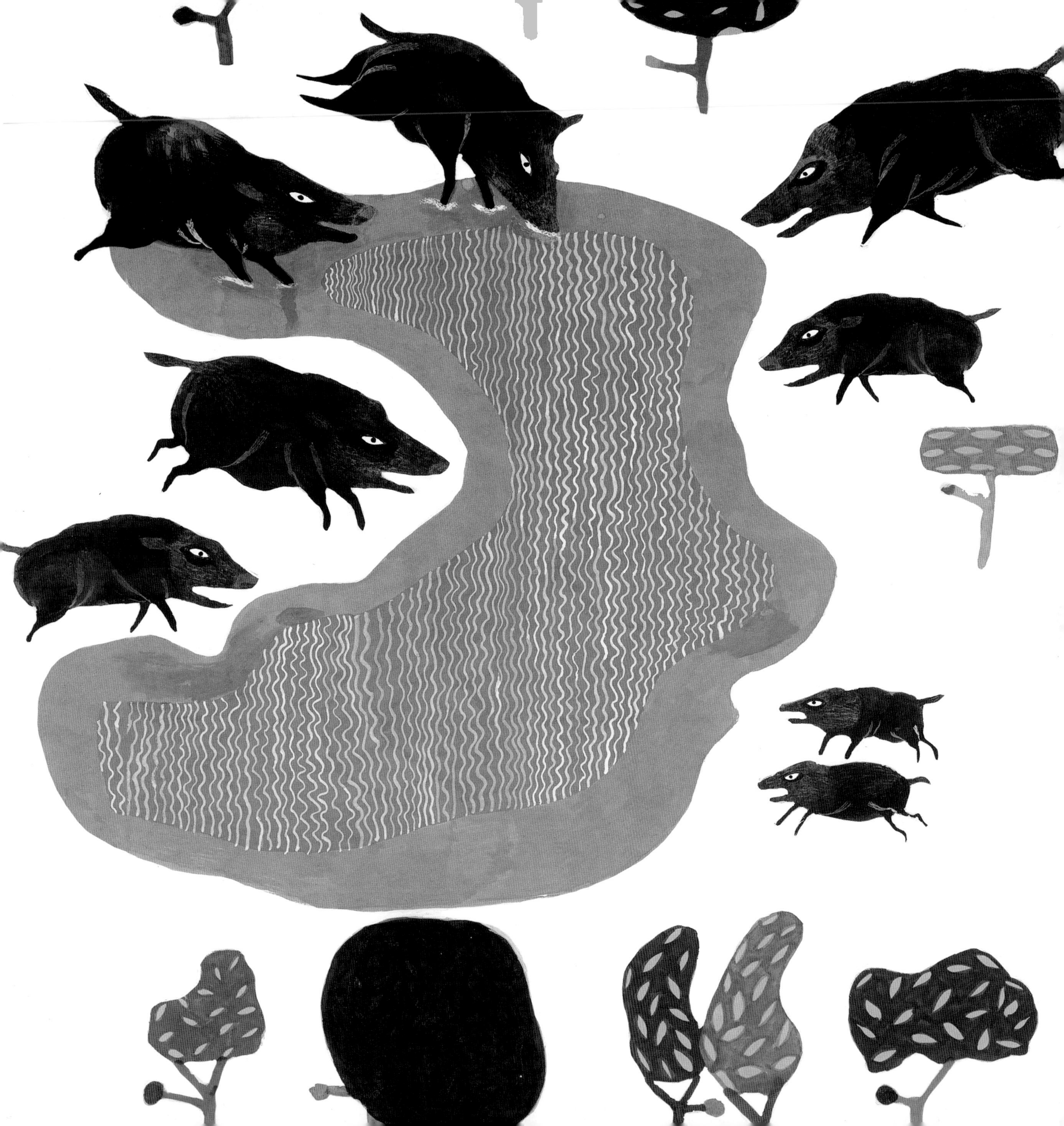

When the task was done, Gorgin was afraid Bijan would tell King Khosrow of his cowardice. So he plotted. He told Bijan there were gardens just over the border, gorgeous beyond all imagining, where lovely girls would gather for a festival. The youth was curious and tempted to explore. He did not know that these were the gardens of the terrible King Afrasaib.

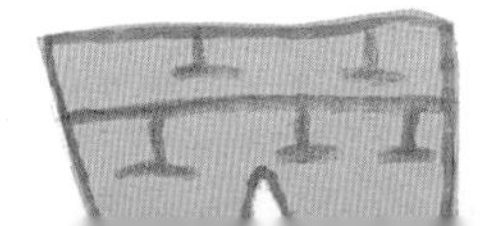

In that beautiful place, he caught sight of Manije at her archery practice, with her bow and arrow, surrounded by her attendants. He fell in love. Manije spied him watching her, and invited the handsome stranger to her tent to talk. But when Bijan learnt who her father was, he refused to put them both in danger by accepting her invitation.

Manije could not bear to lose him and took matters into her own hands. She offered him a drink with a sleeping draft in it. With her maids, she carried the young man to the castle and hid him. There, in secret, Bijan and Manije spent happy days together, learning how to fall more deeply in love.

But palaces have spies, and whispers reached Afrasaib. Bijan was caught and bound. King Afraisab called for his execution, alongside his daughter. Awaiting this fate, Manije begged the king's Vizier, who had been her friend, to save the life of her knight, if not herself. The Vizier, emboldened by his affection for Manije, dared to question the tyrant's order and persuaded the king to lessen their punishment. The princess was banished from the court, and Bijan thrown into a well. A huge rock was dragged over its mouth so he could not escape.

Manije came to the well day after day, bringing Bijan food that she passed through a small gap at the edge of the rock, and building a fire to cook for him and keep herself warm. Meanwhile Gorgin had been full of remorse, and, returning to King Khosrow's court, confessed what had happened. The king and his courtiers were dismayed. Only one man could help. That was Rostam, Iran's greatest knight, its undefeated hero, known for his horned helmet, his blue beard, his superhuman strength and his cunning. The king summoned him.

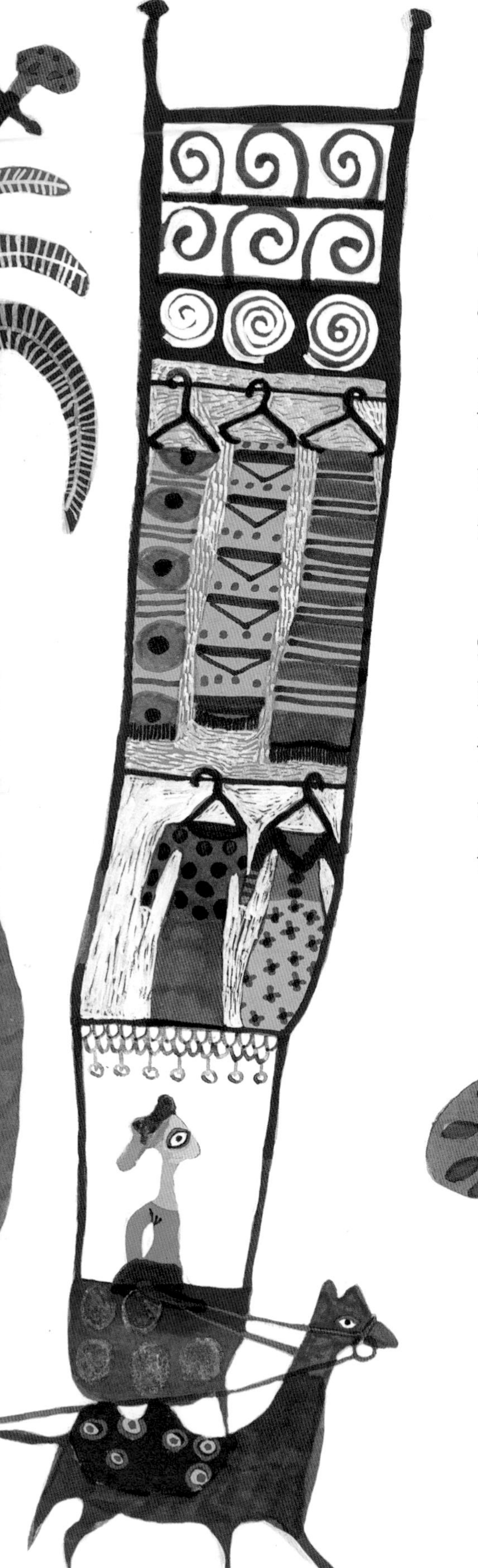

Rostam gathered camels and loaded them with beautifully embroidered clothes, with silks decorated with stars and flowers and stripes, and he rode across the dangerous border disguised as a merchant at the head of a camel train. He found the princess, who told him her sad story. The blue-bearded stranger seemed to take pity on Manije, and made her a present of a chicken to give to the imprisoned knight.

As she served Bijan the bird, she described the man who had given it to her. Hope lit up in Bijan's heart. He knew the horned helmet and the beard. And as he was about to take a mouthful of the chicken, he caught sight of something glinting, and paused. He reached into the flesh. "It is Rostam's ring!" he exclaimed. It was the signal that help was coming.

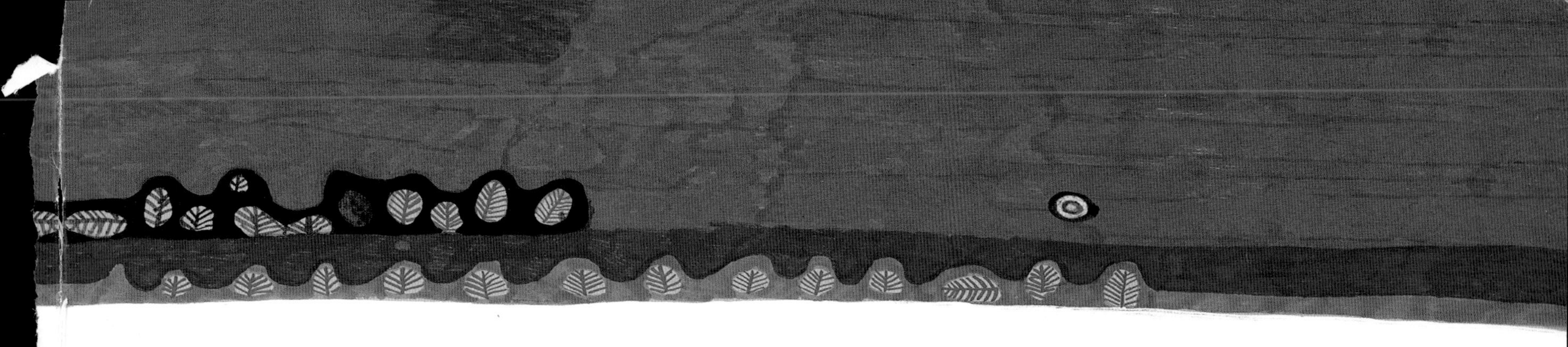

As he spoke, hoofbeats were heard, and riding into view came the mighty Rostam, who leapt from his mount, and, with the strength of several men, heaved the rock from the mouth of the well and hauled the youth out, using Manije's cloak twisted into a rope.

The princess and her knight mounted horses Iran's hero had brought with him and, galloping for their lives, along little trodden paths, the three escaped over the border into the territory of the Armenians, back through the forest, and finally into their homeland, where the sun shone as bright as their spirits.

In Iran they were received with joy. Rostam was the guest of honour at the wedding, but even General Gorgin was invited – after all, it was he who had led Bijan to his bride. And they were so happy to be together, and free, that their hearts were full of forgiveness. Under the shade of a date palm, Bijan and Manije, tested and true, promised each other a happy ever after.

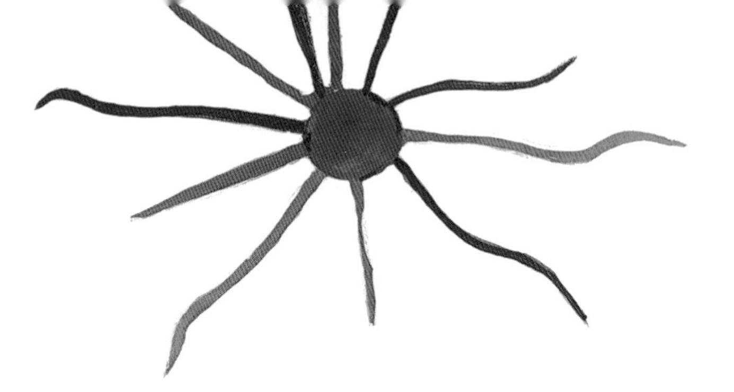

About the book

The story of *Bijan and Manije* is one of the ancient epic stories of *Shahnameh* (Book of Kings). Ferdowsi, the 10th century Persian poet, gathered the historical stories and myths of Persia in the form of poem in *Shahnameh*. The Book of Kings was traditionally the base of Pardekhani, a type of storytelling for the public. They illustrated the stories in large canvas and a narrator read the poems to the audience in coffeehouses and streets, showing them the corresponding illustrations.

Ali Seidabadi has retold the story of *Bijan and Manije* for children. The story is rewritten for English audience by Nicolette Jones. Illustrations are by Marjan Vafaian. Tiny Owl has published *The Parrot and the Merchant* by Marjan before.